The Ant

and the

Big Bad Bully Goat

Andrew Fusek Peters

illustrated by
Anna Wadham

Published by Child's Play (International) Ltd
Swindon   Auburn ME   Sydney

Text © 2007 A. Fusek P...   ...International) Ltd
ISBN 978-1-84643-079...   ...Printed in Croatia

Badger lived in a burrow by the forest.
Everything was just so – his milk jug on the shelf,
a store of honey in the cupboard,
and grain in the kitchen pot.

One fine summer's day, he went into the garden to pick cabbages for his soup. While he was out, a huge, bad old billy goat crept into the burrow and barred the door.

Badger came back to see his door shut tight.
He knocked politely.
Billy Goat answered through the window.
"Your house is all mine now!
It serves you right for leaving it unlocked!"
Badger was angry, but the goat
was bigger and badder than him.

So off he went to see the old bull down the lane, who was feared by all the animals in the village.

"Help me, Bull! Billy Goat has stolen my burrow!"

"You mean Billy Goat with twisty horns
as sharp as swords?" The bull shivered in fear.
"Yes, that's the one!" said Badger.
"Oh, I'm terribly sorry," replied Bull, "but I'm in a bit of a rush.
The farmer has told me to eat all the grass in this field
by sundown. I wish I could be of more help.
Why don't you go and ask Boar?"

On the way past his burrow, Badger heard the goat
tip over his milk jug and slurp up all his milk.

Badger stomped off to see Boar. He was huge
and fierce, with tusks as sharp as crescent moons.
"Help me, Boar! Old Billy Goat has stolen my home!"
"You mean that creature with cloven hooves
that stamp and squash?" whimpered the shaking boar.
"Yes, that's the one!" said Badger.

"I'm…terribly sorry, but I'm on a very important job right now, guarding the forest against trespassers." He grunted loudly, and charged around to show how big and scary he was. "I wish I could be of more help. Why don't you ask Bear?"

On the way past his burrow,
Badger heard Billy Goat smash a jug
and lick up all his honey.

Badger stomped off
to see Bear in her cave.
She towered over Badger.
The claws in her paws
could cut a tree in half.

"Help me, Bear!
Old Billy Goat has stolen my home!"

The ground rumbled as she answered.
"You mean the goat that pushes down
walls, with a head as hard as stone?
"Yes, that's the one!" said Badger.
"Oh, well...you see, I have a lot of jobs
to do before winter, gathering nuts
and berries before my long sleep,
so I can't help you right now.
I'm terribly sorry..."

Badger wandered off
and began to cry.
It was hopeless.

Across his path, there crawled a little ant.
"What's the matter, Badger?"
Badger stopped and studied the bug in the dust.

"Nothing you can help me with, Little Ant!"

"Well, why don't you tell me about it,
and we'll see?" suggested Ant.
Badger told him the whole story,
and Ant came up with a brilliant idea.

"But, my dear Ant, are you quite sure
it will work?" asked Badger.
"We can only try!" said Ant.

Badger nodded, and off they set.

As they approached the burrow, Badger
hid behind a tree. Goat had smashed
open the grain pot, and was busy
stuffing himself. Ant crawled up
the door and through the keyhole.

He climbed onto the table,
and shouted as loud as he could.
"How dare you make such a mess
of Badger's house! Leave right now,
and I will not harm you!"
Goat looked around, unable to see
where the voice was coming from.

He finally spied the little ant, and burst out laughing.
"Listen, little fellow, you're a bit out of your depth here.
Don't you know that I am the big, bad Bully Goat,
with sharp twisty horns, cloven hooves and a head
as hard as stone? Prepare to meet your end!"

"Just wait a second!" replied Ant, bravely.
"My words are sharp enough
to finish you off, you greedy brute!"
"Oh yes? Prove it!" growled Goat.
"Lean closer," shouted Ant, "and feel the sting of my insults!"
Billy Goat leaned closer and at that moment,
Ant stung him right on the nose!

"You see, Goat, size isn't everything!" cried Ant,
leaping up and down in delight.

As for Billy Goat, well, he screamed,
and his nose swelled up so much
he couldn't see a thing.
He blundered around the room,
squeezed through the window,
and fled howling into the night.

Badger ran out from his hiding place to thank Ant
with all his heart. He saw that good things sometimes come
in small packages. Ant and Badger became the best of friends,
and lived together in the burrow for the rest of their days.